The Bone Room

by

Anne Cassidy

First published in 2007 in Great Britain by
Barrington Stoke Ltd
18 Walker St, Edinburgh EH3 7LP

www.barringtonstoke.co.uk

ISBN 978-1-84299-449-8

Printed in Great Britain by Bell & Bain Ltd

A Note from the Author

I love things that can't be explained. An empty cottage with a skeleton ... Why is it there? Would *I* go into the cottage and look at it? Or would I run away? Is it a ghost? Or has it been put there by a criminal to scare people off?

I wanted to write a story about what happens when someone goes into the cottage – to see what they do! And is going into the cottage all they have to do? Is there another, bigger choice they have to make?

And what are all the weird noises in the cottage? What is the story of the skeleton?

I don't know. No one knows.

Contents

Chapter 1
The Canal

Jack Bell walked as fast as he could. He kept his head down and looked at the ground. He was *not* going to look back. If Tony saw him look back, he'd know that Jack was upset. Inside his chest was a ball of anger. Tony was his best mate. How could he show him up again? How could he?

Jack kept going. For a long time. Under his feet the ground went from tarmac to hard pavement. Then it was grass and then it was a path. Jack looked up and saw that he was walking along the canal.

"What's up with you?" he heard someone say.

It was Lulu, the girl who lived next door to him. She stepped onto the path by the canal and Jack had to stop.

"None of your business!" he said.

Lulu, as always, was dressed from head to toe in black.

"Where's Tony?" she said.

"How should I know?" Jack said, and he walked past her quickly.

He went on walking along the canal and left Lulu behind. He knew where Tony was. Still with Josh and Ben. Maybe they were still having a laugh at him. But Tony was *Jack's* mate. How could Tony do that to him?

This afternoon Tony had made Jack really angry. Tony knew Jack was waiting for his birthday to get a new mobile. He knew Jack would pay a lot of money and get the latest model. Even so, Tony had waited until the others were around. Then he'd pointed at Jack's old mobile and said, "Is that your grandad's, mate?"

The others had laughed. It upset Jack even to think about it. He speeded up as if he was in a race. He knew that Tony would turn up at his front door later on. Tony'd try and say it didn't matter.

"Oh, mate! It was only a joke. I didn't know it would upset you!" he'd say.

But Tony did know.

It wasn't Jack's fault if he didn't have much cash. Tony's mum and dad had pots of money. Jack's mum and dad did not. Most of the time he didn't care. He wished that Tony didn't care as well.

Jack slowed down. He took his mobile out of his pocket. Tony was right. It was old and sometimes it didn't work. It weighed a ton as well. What was the point of having a mobile like that? If it didn't work and people took the mickey out of him? What was the point?

Jack stood still for a moment. He looked at the canal and back at his mobile. He turned to walk on, then stopped. He lifted the mobile up and felt how heavy it was. Then, with a sigh, he tossed it in the canal. The mobile sank. He stayed where he was and watched the spot where it went under.

He shook his head and walked on. When he got nearer some old factories he stopped. It was one minute past five. The sky had clouded over and he was feeling chilly. He hugged himself as some swans glided past. They took no notice of him. It began to rain. The drops made spots on the water of the canal. Jack gave another sigh. He was miles from home with no coat. And no mobile. He would get soaked.

Jack thought maybe he'd cut through the factories, onto the road, sprint up and get a bus. But he'd still get wet. Soaked.

Around the side of the factories, further back from the canal, he noticed an old cottage. All the windows had planks nailed across them and were boarded up. Its garden was overgrown. It looked like the other buildings along the canal. Crumbling down and unsafe.

The rain got worse. Jack felt the drops splatter the back of his neck. He turned round to walk back home but it was too far and there was hardly any shelter.

For a moment he didn't know what to do.

He turned towards the cottage. Maybe there was a way in and he could get some shelter for a few minutes. The rain slanted past him and bounced off the ground. Jack ran across to the nearest window. The planks were nailed down. He looked at the front door and saw that there was a padlock on it.

He ran around the side and reached the back garden as the rain speared down. His back was soaked now. Some of the fence was missing and Jack walked into the back garden, through the long grass and overgrown bushes.

The back door was closed. He walked across and took hold of the handle. It opened after a few pulls. He stepped inside, into the inky darkness of the house. He left a gap so that some daylight could get in. He'd wait there until the rain had stopped.

The house smelled old. Jack could taste dust in his mouth. The hallway was narrow and he felt uneasy. He heard something and looked outside to see if anyone was there. The garden was empty. He listened hard.

There was the sound again. Like someone knocking on a door far away. He could just about hear it. It was louder than the noise of the rain slapping down outside.

Jack twisted round. The sound seemed to come from somewhere inside the house. He looked down the black hallway and tried to peer into the dark. He stood totally still, hardly breathing. Nothing. He took a quick look out of the back door. The rain was still hammering down but the sky looked brighter, as if the bad weather was passing over.

Then he heard it again.

Knock, knock, knock.

The sound seemed to come from the floorboards. He could feel it through his legs. He looked down at the floor. Something shot across his feet and startled him.

A mouse. It was only a tiny mouse.

Knock, knock.

Most likely the sound was from a small animal that had got trapped under the floor. Something had crawled in there and couldn't get out.

Knock.

Jack listened hard but it had gone silent. Not a sound. Outside, the rain had stopped as if a tap had been turned off. There was an odd empty silence. Like being under a bridge and waiting for an echo.

It only lasted seconds. Far off he heard some ducks squawk in the canal.

And from deep inside the house the sound of someone crying.

Chapter 2
The Cottage

Jack ran out of the cottage. He stood at the broken fence. He didn't know what to do. Was someone in there? He looked around. There was a narrow alley that led to the road but that was empty. The factories were nearby but they had been shut down years before. It was a funny place to have a cottage – next to all the factories.

But there it was.

It looked empty. It *smelled* empty.

About ten minutes had gone by since he'd heard the sound. A single cry. As if someone had sobbed and stopped. The rain had dried up and the sun was poking through the clouds, making the day feel warm again.

He could call the police. Tell them what he had heard.

What if he was wrong? He'd look stupid. Some teenager who was wasting police time. In any case he couldn't ring the police. He no longer had his mobile. He should go back into the cottage himself. See if anyone was in there.

The cottage only had one floor. Maybe there were just four rooms. He wished Tony was there. Tony would know what to do. Tony'd make a joke of the whole thing. Then it wouldn't seem so serious and Jack could go off home without any worries. But wasn't that what Jack had been angry at Tony for? Making jokes about serious stuff?

He walked to the door.

"Anyone there?" he shouted.

There was no answer. Nothing. He shouted again, a little louder. Again – nothing. The darkness in the hallway was totally still. Not even a mouse this time.

He'd have to go in. Just to be sure that there really was no one in there. He opened the back door as far as it would go so that the light came into the hallway. There was another door on the right and he stepped forward. He turned the handle and pushed the door open. There was enough light to see the edge of a table and something lying on it.

"Anyone around?" he said.

No answer.

He looked again at the table. There was a torch lying there. A torch? Jack took a step into the dark room, picked up the torch and backed out again.

It was heavy and looked new. He pressed the switch and a beam of light sprang out of it. It was odd. The one thing he needed and there it was in front of him. Now he *had* to go into the house and look around. He had no excuse.

Where had the torch come from?

Jack thought about it as he walked up the hallway to the next door. Maybe some kids had been looking around and had left it behind. Or someone from the local council had come to inspect the building.

Jack stood outside the next door. He liked the idea he'd just had. About a man from the council. That meant that someone had looked over the house in the last few days. It made Jack feel better. He had three rooms to look in, then he could go home.

Maybe, when he got home, he'd find that Tony had come round.

He pushed the door open. It was a big room. He moved the torch slowly so that he could see everything from right to left. The light beam showed a bed frame and an old wardrobe. Jack stepped forward to look at the other corner of the room. There was a window with planks across it and what looked like an old rocking chair with a pile of rags stuffed on it.

Nothing else.

He turned to go and then frowned. He swung round and stared hard at the rocking chair. It looked as if there were great big cushions stuffed onto it. It had its back to him and he couldn't see the chair properly. He stepped forward to have a better look.

Then he heard the sound.

Knocking. A soft noise coming from underneath him. He froze and his eyes dropped to the floor.

Knock, knock, knock.

Jack's legs felt wobbly and he edged sideways. He put out his hand and grabbed the wood of the rocking chair for support. It tipped towards him and swung back again and a creaking sound came from its base. Jack tried to take no notice. He pointed his torch at the floor. His mouth felt dry, as if his throat was all tied up in a knot.

"Who's there?" he cried out.

Nothing.

After a few more seconds Jack lifted up the torch and took two steps towards the window. The torch made a bright circle of light around the rocking chair. Jack could see some bulky rags that were stuffed into it.

The chair went on rocking, to and fro, to and fro.

Jack was trembling and the torch was shaking about. He tried to hold it steady and the light beam moved up towards the top of the chair.

His mouth opened in shock. He saw a face. A white face looking at him. Moving closer and back; closer and back, as the chair rocked to and fro.

Jack could feel the blood pounding in his head.

It wasn't a face he could see. It was a skull. Staring at him from among the rags. Jack pushed his back into the wall as hard as it could go. He pulled the torch back and looked into the chair. It wasn't a pile of rags. It was a shirt and jacket. A belt buckle. Cuffs. Fingers.

The hands of a skeleton.

Jack's wrists went weak and he dropped the torch. It rolled away onto the floorboards and its light shone into the far corner of the room.

He was in the dark but he could still see the skull. It was ice white.

Then came the knocking again. Twice. On the floorboards under his feet. As if something might reach up and grab hold of his ankles.

Jack made a sound in his throat and he ran out of the room, along the hallway and burst out into the daylight.

Chapter 3
The Rocking Chair

Jack ran out of the back garden and round to the front of the cottage and the canal. He came to a total stop. The blood was still pounding in his ears and his eyes were squinting in the bright daylight.

Someone in black and all alone was standing by the water. Lulu again, his next-door neighbour. He hardly ever spoke to her. Now it was twice in one day.

"What were you doing in there?" Lulu said.

Jack was panting as if he'd just done a five-kilometre run.

"Are you following me?" he said.

"Don't be stupid. What's in there? You look like you've just seen a ghost."

"What's it to you?" Jack shouted, and walked past her. He was heading for the path by the canal. He wanted to get as far away from the cottage as he could.

He was shaken up, his breath jerky and his hands trembling. What had he seen? What was it? He looked round quickly and saw Lulu a few metres back. He huffed. No one bothered with Lulu. She dressed in a weird way and was rude to everyone. She had a friend from another school who looked the same but was smaller, like a tiny black bird.

Jack passed the factories and thought of the knocking from under the floor as if something was buried there. Buried alive.

The thought of it made him stop for a second. How could he run away if something or someone was buried there? A few moments passed and Lulu was standing by him.

"Something's happened to you."

"No!" he said.

He hadn't seen a ghost. He knew that. But the bones on the rocking chair ...

"My mum told me about that house. It was built in the 1930s by a sailor. It's a listed building. No one can knock it down," Lulu said.

She was walking along beside him.

"Some people say it's haunted."

Jack stopped. "What do you mean?" he said, his skin tingling.

"Just people talking. Could be that people are making it up, but ..." Lulu gave a shrug.

Jack walked up and down. He knocked at his head with his fist.

"What's up?" Lulu said.

He had to think. Was someone playing a trick? Should he go to the police? Or wait and tell Tony? He had to go back to that cottage and find out what the knocking was.

But what if he was wrong? Wouldn't he look a total idiot?

He turned to Lulu. He could tell her. Then if it all came to nothing he could say that she had made it up. No one liked her much.

"You've seen something. In that cottage!" Lulu said.

Jack had to make his mind up. He looked back up the canal path. The cottage was five minutes behind them. He just couldn't walk away.

"Tell me!" Lulu said.

"Want to come and have a look at something in the cottage?" Jack said.

"A ghost?" Lulu said, her mouth open.

"No – it's much worse than that," Jack said, and he had a horrible feeling inside him.

Chapter 4
The Trapdoor

Jack and Lulu stood by the back door of the cottage.

"A skeleton?" Lulu said. She rubbed the collar of the black blouse she was wearing.

"In a rocking chair," Jack said as he looked down the dark hallway.

"That's weird!" she whispered, and smoothed down her hair.

"And the noises," Jack said.

“Ghosts?” Lulu said. She turned to him with a glimmer of excitement in her eyes.

Jack gave a shrug. He looked round. He hoped that no one he knew had seen him with Lulu. He didn’t want to have her there. But he needed her there, as a sort of witness. And *if* it turned out to be nothing, a silly joke maybe, then he could say that he only went in there because she’d asked him to and he’d felt sorry for her. In the back of his mind he could see Tony’s face. How he’d laugh if he knew that Jack was with Lulu.

“Let’s go in,” he said.

She nodded at him. She put her hands together as if she was about to pray.

“You go in front,” Jack said.

She stepped into the hallway. Then she stopped.

“Look,” she said, turning to Jack. “There’s a light coming from the room!”

"It's the torch I dropped," Jack said. He felt glad that it was still there. It meant that no one – or no *thing* – had moved it.

Just then he heard the noise. The knocking. He gripped onto Lulu's arm.

"Ssh," he whispered. "Do you hear it?"

It was stronger this time. Three knocks, far away, coming from underneath them. Lulu turned to him. Her face had a worried look on it. He gave her a little prod and they moved forward until they were both standing outside the room he'd been in before.

The door was still open and the light glowed from inside the room. The light wasn't as bright as it had been before. Maybe the beam from the torch was getting weaker?

"Go in," Jack said, and edged Lulu on.

She stepped ahead into the haze of light from the torch. It seemed to make a blurred halo around her. The rest of the room waited in the dark. There was no sound.

Lulu bent down and picked up the torch. She held it so that it shone up on her face. Then she turned towards the rocking chair.

"Horrible!" she said.

She moved the torch up and down. Jack could see the bones among the old clothes.

"Is all the skeleton there?" she said.

"I don't know. I'm not going to *undress* it!"

The rocking chair was still and Jack made himself look right at the skull. The eye holes were black and deep. It made him feel nervous. As if *something* was staring at him. He had to look down. He looked at the old shirt collar, the jacket, the sleeves. Then his eyes rested on one hand. Its fingers were curled in to make a fist.

Lulu took another step closer. She put out her hand as if she was going to touch the skull. Jack felt himself pulling back.

Then they heard it.

Knock. Knock. Knock.

Right below them.

Lulu pointed the beam of light onto the floor. Jack looked down, his mouth as dry as dust.

"It's under the floorboards," Lulu whispered. "There's something down there!"

She swung the torch from side to side. Jack watched the circle of light move across the floor.

They heard a voice. Someone called out. They said the same word again and again, five, six times. And then a groan as if someone was in pain. Jack's stomach seemed to shrink to the size of a pea. If only he could just leg it out of there. If only he hadn't told Lulu. Now he had to stay.

"There must be a cellar underneath here," Lulu said, her voice louder, her words cracking.

The edge of the light was on the rocking chair, and Jack looked down at the floor and saw something he hadn't noticed before. A thick black line along the floorboards. He leant forward to see what it was.

Lulu was on her knees. She'd put her ear down to the floorboards. She knocked twice on them. A second later there was a knocking sound from below.

"Someone's definitely down there!" she said, looking up.

"Gimme the torch," Jack said.

He directed the light to the space under the rocking chair. There was a line. A thick black line. and it seemed to go along the front of the chair as well as the side.

"It's a trapdoor," Lulu said. She was excited now. "Look, it's underneath the rocking chair."

The knocking went on. Like the beat of a drum. Jack and Lulu stood up. They were looking at the chair, at the skeleton, at the trapdoor underneath it.

"We'll have to move the chair," Lulu said.

Jack put his hands out. He didn't want to touch the skeleton.

"Come on!" Lulu said. "It's dead. It can't hurt you!"

Jack stepped up to the side of the chair. Without looking too closely he grabbed the wooden arm rests and lifted the chair up.

Lulu did the same. The chair wasn't heavy at all. They moved it towards the window so it wasn't sitting over the trapdoor.

Jack shone the torch onto the floor.

In the middle of the trapdoor was a steel ring. Lulu took hold of it and pulled it up towards her. A blast of cold air hit Jack and he backed away. In the hole he could see the beginning of some steps. There was even light down there.

The knocking had stopped. One minute there was just a hole in the floor and then, in a blink of an eye, there was a face. A young girl's face, looking up at him, her skin as white as snow, her eyes dark and full of fear. She scrambled out of the trapdoor and stood in between them. She was tiny, wearing odd clothes. She looked at Jack and then at Lulu.

"Anna?" she said. "Anna? Anna?"

She grabbed Jack's arm and looked around the room. She froze when she saw the skeleton.

Then she started to scream.

Chapter 5
The Cellar

Jack took one arm and Lulu took the other. They pulled the girl out of the house. It wasn't hard. She was very light. At last she stopped screaming. Once they'd got outside, Jack and Lulu let go. The girl almost fell backwards, and Jack grabbed her again. He only just stopped her falling over.

She looked all around. She was frightened.

"Mr Prince is not here?" she said, and looked back at each of them in turn.

Jack gave a shrug. Lulu frowned.

"I have to find Anna," she said. She grabbed Lulu's blouse. She had a strong foreign accent.

"Who is Anna?" Lulu said, softly.

"My sister, Anna. Mr Prince took her!"

"Calm down," Lulu said, "Speak slowly."

The girl was small and pale. Her hair was stringy and looked as if she hadn't brushed it for days. The clothes she was wearing were all creased and crumpled and one arm was black and blue, covered in bruises. The bruises were dark blue and purple, like splashes of paint that someone had tried to wash off. She saw Jack looking.

"Mr Prince hurt me. He says he will hurt Anna. I have to go and find her. I have to go!"

"What's your name?" he said.

"Irena," she snuffled.

"Let's take her back to my house," Lulu said, "We could call the police."

"No police. No police. Mr Prince don't like to call police. *No police!*"

For a small girl she had a loud voice, Jack thought.

"Who's Mr Prince?" Lulu said.

"Mr Prince is bad man. Very bad man. He has taken my sister to circus."

The *circus*. This was crazy. First it was ghosts and skeletons. Now it was a circus.

"He makes her into prostitute!"

"At a circus?" Lulu said with a frown.

Jack's shoulders dropped. A prostitute! What had they got themselves into? At a circus? Then, as if he'd put *circus* into an internet search in his brain, he came up with something.

"Do you mean the Circus *Nightclub*? That's the new place that opened a few months ago. In town."

"I know where you mean!" Lulu said.

"Where is town?" Irena said. She looked all around, as if she might be able to see it.

"It's up the road," Lulu said. She pointed past the factories. "But it's a long way up the road."

"I have to go now," Irena said. "If Mr Prince comes here and I am not in cellar," she pointed at the ground, "then he will hurt Anna. He can do it. I must go to circus and find Anna."

She turned to go.

"Wait," Lulu said. She looked over at Jack. "You won't find her on your own. We'll help you. But you must tell us what's happened to you. Where do you come from? How did you get here?"

Irena gave a long sigh.

"We are from Russia. We give our money to man in our village. He put us on coach and then boat, and then we land in England. Mr Prince takes us onto small boat and we get off here. Three, maybe two days ago. Mr Prince says he has job for us."

"He smuggled you into this country," Jack whispered.

"Now we must go. We must get Anna," Irena said.

Lulu looked at Jack again.

"We really should ring the police!" he said.

"No police. *No police!*" Irena said. She grabbed Lulu's hand. She shook her head. Her eyes looked wild.

"All right, all right," Lulu said.

"My bag. My bag is in cellar!" Irena said. Her face went red and she looked as if she was about to cry. "I can't go back in house. I can't!"

Jack looked at the old cottage and thought of the room in the ground and the bones in the rocking chair. At least now he knew it wasn't a ghost.

"Don't worry. I'll go and get it," he said.

He clicked the torch on and walked up the hallway. When he went into the room he turned it off. The electric light coming out from the cellar was enough to see by. He looked in the trapdoor. There were the steps. He turned round and put his foot on the first step and went down.

The cellar was a small room. It was the size of a bathroom but there was no toilet or washbasin. And no door that led to one. It didn't smell very good. Then he noticed the bucket with the lid in the corner. He turned away. It made him feel sick. Opposite were some sleeping bags and cushions. In the other corner was a plastic box with six or seven bottles of water and what looked like packets of biscuits.

The room felt damp. He thought about how the water from the canal might seep through the earth towards it. It gave him a shudder.

He saw a rucksack in between the sleeping bags. It had a red sparkling heart sewn on it. On the zip was a tangle of beads and a couple of feathers. He picked it up. There was a strong smell of perfume coming from it.

He left the light on and went up the steps. The air felt chilly, as if the weather had turned cold. He went on up until his head was in the room above and his body was still on the steps. It felt odd to have his face in darkness but the rest of him in light. He clicked the torch on and it gave off a weak beam. The room was cooler than before, he was sure. He went up the last three steps and stood in the room. The girl's rucksack hung down his back and the feathers tickled his arm. He clicked off the torch.

It had got colder. Jack rubbed his arms with his hands.

He bent down and pulled the trapdoor towards him. He shut it and cut off the light that came up from below. It didn't matter about the dark. He would be outside in a moment.

He heard a noise. A creaking noise.

He looked round the room and listened hard. He thought he heard Lulu's voice from out the back of the cottage but nothing else.

He stood up and dusted off his jeans. There was the noise again. A creak. Distant, far away. Like a child's swing going to and fro.

Jack stepped away from the trapdoor. He looked into each dark corner. He remembered he had the torch and clicked it on. Its light wavered over the room and Jack had a quick sight of the back of the rocking chair. Then the torch battery died and the room sunk into blackness.

He swore.

The *sound* was still there. Far away, as if it came from another room in another house. A low squeak, a chair that swung back and forth. And yet, when he closed his eyes for a moment, the cold seemed to curl around him and the sound was there in the room just behind his ear.

The rocking chair – forwards and backwards. A creak and a moan.

Fear pinned him to the spot. He could not move. Then the noise stopped, suddenly, and the room felt bigger and emptier and as silent as a church. Jack opened his eyes and edged away towards the door. He felt for the door frame and then turned and walked quickly up the hall and out into the back garden. The light hit him and he felt like he was looking right into the sun.

"You all right?" Lulu said. Her black clothes made her look as if she was at a funeral.

He didn't answer. He looked down and made himself busy with dusting Irena's bag off. His thoughts were all in a tangle.

"Irena needed a pee. She's gone round the side of the factory. Near those bushes. That her bag?"

"Well, it's not mine!" Jack said, and put it on the ground. He walked away from it.

All at once, he felt fed up. What had he been dragged into? He was stuck with Lulu and this foreign girl who was in some odd sort of trouble. Why him? Why couldn't he have kept out of it? What would Tony say if he knew?

"She's been gone a long time," Lulu said, after a few moments.

"I'm not going to check!" Jack said.

"I'll go," Lulu muttered.

Lulu walked towards the old factory. Her black skirts billowed out until she'd vanished round the corner. Seconds later she came running back.

"I can't see her anywhere," Lulu shouted. "She must have run off towards town."

The girl had gone. Maybe it was for the best, Jack thought, looking round. He looked back at the planks over the windows of the empty cottage.

Chapter 6
The Road to Town

Lulu was upset.

"We should follow her," she said.

"Why?" Jack asked. He'd had enough. "Let her go."

"She's in trouble!" Lulu said.

"She's breaking the law," Jack replied. "She shouldn't even be in this country!"

Jack was going home. He was fed up. Maybe Tony had called for him while he was out. He hadn't asked for any of this. The scruffy girl from Russia. The cottage with its odd noises. The rocking chair and the bones. He just wanted to leave it behind.

"She's not a criminal," Lulu went on.

"Some people would say she is," Jack said. "She's broken the law. She's an illegal immigrant!"

"She's done nothing bad," Lulu said. "Her and her sister trusted someone to get them a job. Instead they've been kidnapped!"

"The police will deal with it," Jack muttered.

"Then the girls will end up in prison. They'll be deported," Lulu's voice was getting louder.

Jack peered out of the broken fence. It wasn't any of his business. When he turned back he saw the silly rucksack on the grass. The feathers were blowing in the breeze. The pink heart looked like it had been sewn on by hand. It made him feel sad. He didn't know why.

"What if it was your sister?" Lulu asked.

"I haven't got a sister," Jack said.

"That's not the point," Lulu replied. "Are you coming? I'm going after her. We'll lose her if we don't go now."

Jack closed his eyes and picked up the rucksack. He was cross now. He followed Lulu as she raced up the factory alley and out onto the road. They stopped on the pavement and looked up and down. In one direction the road went towards the canal. In the other it headed uphill towards the town, passing some old boat yards and warehouses.

"There she is," Lulu said.

Jack looked. Far ahead he could see Irena walking up towards the main road.

"Come on," Lulu said. "We'll catch her up. She'll get lost without us."

Lulu sprinted off. She ran faster than Jack expected. Her black skirts flew out around her. He jogged behind. He felt silly with the girl's bag over his arm and the feathers fanning out as he went along.

Lulu seemed to be going faster. Jack fell back a bit, the sun heavy on his back. The road was so steep, it slowed him down. Up in front Irena seemed just as far away. Then she stopped. She stood still with her hands on her hips and looked like she was out of breath. Lulu called to her, "Wait for us!" and slowed down. In a few steps Jack caught up with Lulu, gave a little wave to Irena and pointed at the rucksack. Irena nodded.

A car turned off the main road. A big dark SUV. It looked new and expensive and was out of place in among the run-down buildings and closed-up shops. Its windows were tinted and there was a thud of music as it sped past them towards the canal. A few seconds later Jack heard a screech. He spun round to look as the SUV did a jerky three-point turn and sped back up the road back the way it had just come. It passed them in a flash and seemed in a hurry to get away. But moments later it made a sudden stop alongside Irena. That was when Jack saw the number plate – PR1 NC3.

The driver's door flew open and a man got out. He was big and had a ponytail.

"Oh, no," Lulu said.

The music spilled out of the car as the man took two or three steps and grabbed hold of Irena. With one hand he opened the passenger door and with the other he pushed her in. Jack thought he heard a squeal. He started to run towards the car, with Lulu following him.

It was too late. The car revved up and moved up the road fast. In a moment it was gone.

"That was Mr Prince!" Lulu said.

Jack stopped. He felt hopeless and helpless. He hadn't wanted to be a part of this, hadn't wanted to get involved. But now that he'd seen the size of the man, the size of his car, the loudness of his music, the way he'd snatched up Irena, Jack knew he had to do something.

"Now what?" Lulu said.

"The Circus nightclub," Jack said. "That's where he'll take her."

A bus came along and they jumped on it. It only took five minutes and they were in town.

As Jack was getting off the bus he saw the club. It was on the end of a row of shops. Further along, parked half up on the pavement, was the SUV. He could see the registration PR1 NC3. This had to be the right place. Jack gave a sigh, picked up the rucksack, and followed Lulu.

Chapter 7
The Circus Club

The Circus Club was a shop that had shut down some years before. The outside looked like it was made of marble but, when Jack touched it, he knew it was just a stick-on covering. There were no windows, only a set of double swing doors that were closed. Beside them was a small gold plate. *THE CIRCUS CLUB – Members Only*, it said.

"Is it a strip club?" Lulu said. She screwed her nose up.

Jack gave a shrug. He did know a bit about the club. He'd read something in the local paper. It was a twenty-four-hour pub and it was mostly men that went there. It had snooker and cable television and exotic dancers. Local people wanted to have it closed down. They said it would bring crime to the area.

Just then one of the swing doors opened and Mr Prince burst out. Jack made eye contact with the man for a second. Then he hooked Lulu's arm into his as if they were walking on, past the club. Close up the man was really big. He was talking into a mobile phone and Jack could see that he had metal on his teeth. As if he was wearing a brace. He listened as the man walked by. He had a posh accent, like royalty. Funny, with his name being Mr Prince! *Why should he be* Mister *Prince?* Jack thought. *He didn't deserve that kind of respect.*

Jack remembered Irena's rucksack. The pink heart and the feathers felt bigger and brighter to him suddenly. He quickly put the rucksack on his other arm so Prince wouldn't see it.

They walked on past and didn't look back. Then Jack heard a car door slam and the engine revving. He looked round and saw the SUV drop off the pavement and drive away.

"Let's go round the back," Lulu said. "We might find a way in."

They walked round the corner until they came to a brick wall with a wooden door. A sign on it said, *The Circus Club – Deliveries*. Lulu pushed at it and it swung back. They stepped into the yard. It was tiny and had crates stacked as high as the wall. The back door of the club was hanging open. Jack looked in. There were some stairs to the right and a hallway which led straight through to the bar. There was loud music playing, and some flashing lights. He saw a group of men drinking from bottles and beyond them he could see a snooker table.

"We could go in, upstairs, and see if the girls are there," Lulu whispered in his ear.

Jack looked at the stairs. He wasn't sure.

"Come on, while that big bloke is away," Lulu said.

He waited. He didn't know what to do. They should just ring the police and let them sort it out.

"Oh, I'll go first!" Lulu hissed and before Jack could open his mouth, she was half-way up the stairs. After a moment, he followed her.

There was a landing and three doors. The stairs went on up to another floor but Lulu was trying all the doors. One was an office, the second led to an empty bedroom, the third to a tiny room full of cardboard boxes.

“Come on!” Lulu said.

She went up the second flight of stairs. Jack looked down the stairs and into the stairwell. He ducked back as he saw someone’s head pass by on the stairs below. He watched Lulu’s skirt puffing out in front of him and followed her up. At the top there was only one door. On the outside was a bolt. Lulu pulled it back and pushed the door open.

Two girls sat on a bed in an attic room. One of them was Irena.

“Thank goodness we found you!” Lulu said and walked across to the bed.

The other girl was bigger than Irena and looked younger. She must have been Anna. She was wearing a lot of make-up, with heavy black on her eyes, and her lips were red and glossy. She had a short skirt on and high heels. Her top was sparkly and very low. Jack could see a lot of her breasts. He looked away. He felt embarrassed. On the floor, by the bed, was a blue rucksack with a pink heart sewn on it and a feather tied onto the zip. Jack put Irena's rucksack down beside it.

Anna stood up. She was taller than Jack and Lulu.

"We have to go from here! You can help us?"

"The police would help ..." Jack said. He was starting to sound like a recording.

Anna and Irena shook their heads.

"Police will send us back to Russia. We have no home left in Russia. We want to go to our uncle in London. This is why we came! This is why we pay Mr Prince our money!"

Jack looked at Lulu. It wasn't up to him to decide.

"Please, help us to go to London. We have address!"

"Let's get out of here," Lulu said. "Then we can decide what to do. You go first, Jack. Make sure there's no one about."

Jack walked out onto the landing. The girls picked up their rucksacks and followed him. Lulu was last.

He looked down the stairs, over the banister. There was no one down there that he could see. The four of them walked down the first flight of stairs. They didn't make a sound. When they got to the middle landing Jack made a sign at them to them to stand back. He leant over the banister and looked down again. There was nothing. Just sounds – music, talk, the click of snooker balls. He started to walk down the stairs. Anna was behind him.

When he was half-way down Jack heard a voice coming from the back yard. A posh voice, like royalty.

"Don't worry, old boy. I have the girls here and I'm picking up the other one tonight."

Jack looked round. Anna's face was full of fear. She turned and went back up the stairs. Prince was still talking.

"Don't worry. They'll do it. They have no choice. When I get the new girl you'll have three. Then you can pay me!"

Jack followed Anna up. Prince was talking as if he was going to *sell* the girls. Like they were slaves. He had to get them away. He whispered something to Lulu. She nodded and opened one of the room doors and took the girls in.

Jack walked slowly down the stairs. When he got to the bottom he stood in full view and looked at Prince, who was just finishing his phone call.

"Who are you? What are you doing in here?" Prince shouted.

"There's a sick girl upstairs. She's bleeding. You should call an ambulance."

"What?"

Prince side-stepped Jack and half-walked, half-ran up the stairs. Jack followed a few steps behind. The big man was puffing by the time he got to the top. Jack was almost behind him as he went into the attic room. As soon as he was in, Jack closed the door and pulled the bolt across it. There was a second of silence and then Prince started to shout and swear.

Jack ran downstairs and banged on the girls' door. "Come on!"

They followed him down the stairs and out into the yard. They kept running for a few minutes and then stood on a corner, each of them panting hard as if they'd just run a race.

"Now what?" Anna said. Her breasts looked like tiny balloons bursting out of her top. Jack looked away.

"We take you to the station. You can get a train to London. Right, Jack?" Lulu said.

Jack nodded. They had almost been sold as slaves. They deserved a bit of luck. Why not?

Chapter 8
The Station

They sat in the café at the station. The sisters were drinking Cokes. Anna had bought tickets for the 7.40 train to London.

"Will you be all right? When you get to London?" Lulu said.

"We have address," Anna said in a firm voice.

Anna had changed her clothes in the women's toilets. She was wearing jeans and trainers and a T-shirt. Now that he couldn't see her breasts, Jack could look straight at her.

"What did Prince mean about the new girl?" Jack said.

"He has another girl coming tonight," Irena said. "She is Russian. He picks her up from docks at eleven. He will put her in cellar."

"We should call the police," Lulu said.

Jack was glad that Lulu had said it this time. Anna shook her head.

"Mr Prince is very clever. He sees police near cottage, he just make boat go on. He will take girl to some other place. It is hard to catch Mr Prince. He has many places."

They saw the sisters onto their platform. Jack watched for a moment as they walked off. He noticed that the feathers on their rucksacks looked more springy. He wondered if they would be all right in London.

On the bus Jack sat forward and used his fists to knock at his head. He made a decision.

"I'm going to go to the cottage and wait for Prince. When he turns up, with the new girl, *then* I'll call the police."

"I've been thinking that myself," Lulu said. "We'll catch him red-handed."

"You're not coming!" Jack said. "I'm doing this on my own!"

"I'm coming. We've been in this together. I'm not stopping now. I want to see Prince get caught just as much as you do."

Jack said nothing. There was no point in arguing. He had learned that much about Lulu.

Chapter 9
The Boat

It was pitch dark by the time Jack and Lulu got to the canal.

Lulu clicked on the torch. She had borrowed this one from her dad's toolbox. It made a sharp circle of light on the canal path in front of them. Everywhere else looked black. The water was still. There were no boats that he could see. Jack could hear some traffic from the road.

“Not far now,” Jack said. He could see the shapes of the old factories up ahead of him.

“What time is it?” Lulu asked.

“Almost eleven. If Prince is picking the girl up at the docks at eleven, he won’t get here till about midnight. We’ve got plenty of time. What did you tell your mum and dad?”

“I said I was staying over at my mate’s.”

“Me too,” Jack said. He wished he was.

He wished he *was* staying over at Tony’s. They’d be watching movies, having a laugh, eating some takeaway. Instead he was here with Lulu.

When they got to the cottage Jack was puzzled. The cottage wasn’t in the dark. Lulu turned off the torch. The factories had some security lights which spilled over and gave a faint yellow glow to everything around.

"It looks spooky at night," Lulu said. "No wonder people said there was a ghost."

They went round the back of the cottage and walked through the gap in the fence. Jack crossed to the back door. He pulled it open. The hallway was dark and looked like it went on forever, like a hole in the ground. Lulu clicked on the torch again. Jack could see the door to the kitchen and the far door to the room where the rocking chair was. He swallowed a couple of times. It had been hard to go in there in daylight but it seemed much, much worse at night.

He stepped into the hallway and walked slowly up to the far door. With one hand he pushed the door open. The torch lit up the corner of the room and Lulu moved the light around until they could see the back of the rocking chair. Jack walked across and made himself turn the chair around. He looked right at the bones. The skull stared back at him.

"Just a pile of old bones," Lulu said.

He bent over and pulled up the trapdoor. The light came out, giving the room a honey colour. He looked down. There was no one there. Everything was just as they had left it that afternoon.

Jack remembered then the odd noise he'd heard. He listened for a moment but there was just silence. It felt like they were deep underground.

"We'll wait outside, by the factory wall," he said. "Then, when the boat comes, we can call the police."

But Lulu wasn't listening. She'd put her finger on her lips to tell Jack to shut up. There was a noise coming from outside. Jack looked at his watch. It was only 11.15. Prince couldn't have got here so soon. Jack opened his mouth to say something but then heard voices from outside. One male voice and one female.

Lulu turned the torch off and they both stood back against the wall. The voices were coming from the front of the cottage, on the other side of the boarded-up window. Jack looked in that direction. There was a thin strip of light coming through the planks on the windows. It must mean that there was a gap. Jack crept towards it and looked out.

He could see two people. His heart sank. One of them was Prince. He was walking back towards the canal, and there was a girl standing close to the window. She was tall with blonde hair. It wasn't cold but she was hugging herself. Beyond her Jack could see the boat. It was small and dark. It must have slipped through the water without a sound.

Jack stepped back from the window and tugged Lulu's arm. They went out of the room and down the hall to the back door. They stood outside. Lulu had her mobile out and was jabbing at the buttons.

"Oh, no!" she whispered.

"What?"

"I've got no battery. I don't get it!"

"How can you have no battery? Didn't you check?"

"I always have battery. I charge it every night," she hissed. "You ring. Use your mobile."

But Jack's mobile was in the canal.

"I haven't got it," he said. He felt useless.

Lulu sank down by the wall. Then after a moment she stood up again and her face became hard and firm.

"You stay here. I'll go and find a call box," she said. "There'll be one up the road."

Jack nodded. He took the torch from her.

Lulu swept across the garden. Her dark clothes flapped out like the wings of a bird.

Then she was gone. Jack stood by the back door. He kept his head close up to the door frame. Just then the front door creaked open and the light from the old factories spilled into the cottage.

The girl walked in first. Behind her was Prince with some bags. He spoke to the girl in another language. They both went into the room with the trapdoor.

Jack looked round. It was dark but everything had a creepy yellow glow.

He hoped Lulu would find a call box.

Chapter 10
The Skeleton

Jack heard loud, angry voices from inside the cottage. At first they were both at the same volume. Then the girl's voice got softer and Prince's got louder. There was some crying, and then a bang.

He guessed that the trapdoor had been shut. He felt a twist of anger in his stomach. He stood back against the brick wall. What would Prince do now? He listened. He heard a door open and footsteps moving away towards the front of the cottage. Prince was going out.

Jack heard the front door close and he waited for a moment. Then he opened the back door a tiny bit and looked in. There was no one there. All he could hear was the crying of the girl coming from under the floor.

It had been the same that afternoon when he'd first stepped into the cottage. But this time the crying got louder. Angry, scared sobs. It made Jack's stomach flutter. He had to help her, to get her out. Maybe Lulu had already rung for the police.

He walked quickly into the house. He went into the room and turned his torch on. On the floor were some bags. From below he could hear the girl. She sounded desperate. Did she know about Prince now? Did she know the sort of *job* Prince had set up for her?

Jack knelt down by the trapdoor. He was about to pull it open when he saw something on the floor. He put his hand out for it. It was a bunch of keys with a large P attached to them. At that moment Jack heard the front door rattle. Then it opened and Jack heard footsteps coming back up the hall. He stood up, his heart thudding. Prince had dropped his car keys and now he'd come back for them. Jack hadn't had enough time to get the girl out. Now it was too late. Prince would come in and find him there. He felt as if his stomach had dropped down into his knees.

A ring tone sounded. Then Prince's voice. Prince stood still, on the other side of the wall, talking into his mobile. Jack looked around. He began to panic. Where could he hide? Then he noticed the old wardrobe up against the far wall. Without a second thought he clicked the torch off and stepped across to it as silently as he could. He held his breath and turned the handles. The two doors opened outwards. Not a sound. Not even a tiny creak. He got inside and pulled the doors towards him just as Prince walked into the room. Prince was still talking loudly into his mobile. Jack let his breath out slowly and silently.

From inside the wardrobe Jack could hear Prince marching back and forth in the room. He was speaking in another language. His words were short and stuttering. Jack pushed one of the doors open one or two centimetres. It was dark but he could make out Prince hitting the air with the back of his hand. Then Prince cut the call. The girl was shouting loudly from down in the cellar. It seemed to make Prince mad and he shouted back. In a temper, he pushed the rocking chair so that it skidded backwards across the floor and stopped in the far corner of the room. Then he kicked the girl's bags out of the way.

Prince bent down. Jack heard the clink of keys and a clunk as the trapdoor opened.

Yellow light came out of the cellar. Prince shouted. Jack could hear the girl coming up the stairs. She spoke loudly. Her words were spilling out, half-crying, half-angry. She got out of the cellar and tried to move away from Prince but he held onto her. She argued with him, her voice full of anger.

Without warning, Prince grabbed her by her blouse and pulled her up towards him. He was talking in a low voice, and in another language. Jack didn't know what he was saying but he knew Prince was threatening the girl. The girl went limp and whimpered.

Jack's mouth went dry and he began to feel cold, his skin chilled. He edged the other wardrobe door open. Prince was backing the girl up to the wall. One of his hands was up in the air, as if he was going to hit her. Jack thought, *I must get out.* He knew he was no match for Prince but he knew too that he should get out and help the girl.

Then he heard another noise. A creak.

It was a sound like a swing going to and fro. He remembered it from before – from the afternoon. Jack licked his lips and looked into the room. The rocking chair was over in the corner. It looked odd. For a moment Jack thought he saw it *rocking*. He closed his eyes and opened them again. The light from the cellar was dim. Jack couldn't see properly.

Prince had his back to Jack. He was talking fast at the girl. His words sounded sharp and angry but in between there was softness, as if he was promising her something. Without warning she suddenly screamed, and Prince lifted his hand up and slapped her face. Jack flinched at the sound. He let the wardrobe doors swing open and stepped out.

Prince spun round.

“You!” he said.

Jack should have been afraid of Prince but he wasn’t even looking at him. Instead he stood still and stared into the far corner of the room. Was he seeing things? The rocking chair was *moving*. It was tipping backwards and forwards.

Prince grabbed him and threw him towards the girl.

Jack didn’t feel a thing. He kept looking at the rocking chair and trying to see the bones, the fingers sticking out of the sleeves. But it was just too hard to see. The yellow light from the cellar seemed to move towards the chair like a mist. Could Jack see it rocking? Or was it that he could just hear it groaning backwards and forwards?

Prince turned and looked.

“Oh, no,” he said.

The girl gasped. Jack stood stock still.

A shape formed. Ice white. A blur. The chair creaked. Back and forth, back and forth. Jack felt himself go weak, his legs felt like rubber. When he blinked there was just yellow light but then in a moment it was there again, a white mask. A skull. Staring at them.

Prince was muttering something. He fell to his knees. The chair moaned softly as it rocked. Jack heard Prince praying out loud. The same line over and over. Like a chant. Jack listened and drew his breath in spoonfuls. The girl had grabbed hold of him. He could feel her nails digging into the skin on his arm.

The skull rocked to and fro. Its black eyes were full of sadness.

Then it was gone.

All Jack could see was a pile of rags and bones.

From outside somewhere he could hear a siren. Over and over. Coming closer. The police. At last.

Prince stood up and looked around. He seemed in a daze. He swore at Jack and shoved him and the girl across the room. He took one last look at the rocking chair, then he turned and marched out of the room. Jack could hear the clink of the car keys and the front door slam.

Chapter 11
The Bone Room

The police put the sobbing girl in their car and got on their radios for help to follow Prince. Lulu got in beside her.

"It's a black SUV. Registration number PR1 NC3," Jack said.

"If we get off now, we might see him," the officer said. He repeated what Jack had said into a radio. Then he turned to Jack. "You wait here. A squad car's on its way, five minutes tops. Then you can make your statements at the station and we'll take you home. You've done a good job here."

Lulu waved. Jack gave a shaky smile. He was glad it was over and yet he was trembling. He needed to sit down. His ears were ringing and his head hurt. He leant on the old factory wall as the police car drove off. The police had turned off the siren but the blue light was flashing. The police car looked odd, Jack thought, as if it was in a film with the sound turned down.

Jack still had Lulu's dad's torch in his hands.

He looked down at his watch. It was gone midnight. He looked up the road which was now empty. He turned and looked back at the cottage. It was still, like a picture. The yellow light from the factories hung around it. Nothing moved, not so much as a mouse. He walked towards the gap in the fence and went through to the back door. He stood by it, looking into the black hallway.

What had he seen in that room? The room where the bones were?

He had heard a noise, he had seen movement, there had been something. A face? Was it a trick of the light that had shone up from the cellar? What were those bones in the chair?

Jack peeked in the door. Was there a creaking sound? A swing moving to and fro? He concentrated. Every brain cell he had was alert.

But in the hallway there was a hush. The cottage had sunk into silence. Jack clicked the torch on and looked at the circle of light on the floorboards. It made the darkness seem thicker and more heavy. He felt his neck tingle. Would he ever know what had really happened?

He banged his fist on his head. He couldn't just walk away.

He clicked the torch on, walked along the hallway and went into the room. The trapdoor was shut and the room was black. He stood for a moment. What should he do now? He aimed the torch into the corner.

The rocking chair had its back to him.

He stepped across and pulled the corner of it so that it turned slowly round.

Just bones.

He aimed the torch at the skull. He stared into the eye sockets. Had there been something there? Sadness? Anger? He put his fingers out to touch the cheekbone. It felt dry and delicate. Was it a skeleton? Or was it just bones stuffed into old cushions and rags, like a guy on top of a bonfire?

In the back of his head he heard the police siren. It was like a wailing bird far away, coming closer. Jack did a slow circle and looked round the room.

Just cobwebs and dust.

He walked out into the night. The siren was louder, near by. He left the back garden and went along the alley. Up in front, at the end, he saw a blue light flashing on and off.

For a moment he thought he heard a noise. A creak, a groan. He stopped. Part of him wanted to turn round and look back. Instead he kept looking at the blue light; on and off, on and off, on and off.

"All right, son?" a policeman shouted.

He would not turn round.

He waved at the officer and walked towards them.

Barrington Stoke would like to thank all its readers for commenting on the manuscript before publication and in particular:

Scott Angel
Christopher Andrews
Sam Beck
Josh Bond
Rianne Bowler
Ollie Coggins
Mrs S. Gillespie
David Henderson
Laura Lee
Sophie Lennon
Hannah Nutting
Laura Organ
Megan Rose
Sam Shead
Tahnee Smith
Shona Thomson
Clive Williams

Become a Consultant!

Would you like to give us feedback on our titles before they are published? Contact us at the email address below – we'd love to hear from you!

info@barringtonstoke.co.uk
www.barringtonstoke.co.uk

If you liked this book, why don't you try ...

Shadow on the Stairs

by Ann Halam

Every night Joe looks for the shadow on the attic stairs. Sometimes he thinks he can see it. Sometimes he's sure it's in his mind. But nothing can prepare Joe for the terrible night when he finds out what the shadow really is ...

If you liked this book, why don't you try ...

Bloodline

by Kevin Brooks

It's Saturday morning and Finbar Black is spending the day at his dad's. There's no reason to think it will be any less boring that usual, but when a crazy girl bursts into the house, with a gun and a bag full of cash, Finbar's day is suddenly turned upside down. Who is this beautiful stranger? What has she done? And how can she possibly get away with it?

If you liked this book, why don't you try ...

Kill Swap

by James Lovegrove

A boy with a *big* problem.

A man who says he has the answer.

Darkness. A gun. Somebody about to die.

The nightmare has just become real ...

If you liked this book, why don't you try ...

Prisoner in Alcatraz

by Theresa Breslin

It is your right to have: food, clothing, shelter and medical attention.

Anything else you get is a privilege.

Marty is doing life in the hardest prison in America. No-one gets out of Alcatraz. But now there's a new escape plan. Can Marty break out of Alcatraz – or will life mean life?